Dani Banani
Talented Train Driver

Written by Lisa Rajan
Illustrated by Alessia Trunfio

Collins

Chapter 1

Dani Binns opened the door of the spare bedroom.

"It's toy box time!" she told her sister Tara, excitedly.

Every time she chose a toy from the box, she was sent off on an adventure and given a job to try out. *What will I be today?* she wondered.

She took out a microphone.

Perhaps I'll be a news reporter? she thought.

Her hand began to tingle. The tingling spread up her arm and around her whole body. Then she began spinning and tumbling through space and time …

Chapter 2

When the spinning stopped, Dani found herself on the platform at a busy railway station. *Am I catching the train somewhere?* she wondered.

"All aboard, please ... the train is about to depart!" shouted the conductor from the cab near the front. "You too, Dani – you're the driver!"

"I'm Tai," he said. "This is Asha. She'll show you how everything works."

"Why have you brought a microphone?" Asha asked. "You're driving the train, not making announcements! Here's your uniform."

The signal turned green and Dani pulled the lever to get the train moving. It glided forward, getting faster every second.

"Is this too fast?" asked Dani, feeling unsure.

"No, this is a good speed," Asha replied. "We have to get these passengers to the next station on time. We can't be late!"

Suddenly, Dani saw something in the distance up ahead. Oh no! There was a herd of cows on the track! She blasted the horn. HONNNK!

Dani was terrified. She pushed the brake lever as hard as she could and held her breath. *Will the train stop in time?* she panicked.

The train screeched to a halt just before it reached the herd. *Phew!*

The noise had disturbed the cows. They began walking towards the open gate that led into their field. All except one, who was munching the juicy grass beside the track. It wasn't moving.

Dani blasted the horn again. The cow kept chewing.

"Can we jump down and shoo the cow away?" asked Dani.

"No," said Tai, "the safest place is on the train. We'll just have to wait till it moves. I'll tell the passengers why we've stopped."

"But we can't wait too long …" began Asha nervously.

"Why?" asked Dani.

Chapter 3

"Trains use this track in both directions. There's a train coming the other way very soon!" blurted Asha. "The driver won't expect us to still be here."

"What should we do?" asked Dani, panic rising.

"Radio the signaller," said Asha. "Quickly!"

Dani called the signaller and explained what had happened.

"This is an emergency call. Make sure the signal is red," she requested, "so that the other train won't hit us … or the cow!"

"The signal is red," came the reply. "Find a way to move that cow … and fast. The intercity express can't be delayed!"

Asha shouted out of the window. The cow ignored her. Maybe it couldn't hear her.

The other cows went through the gate. One of them mooed loudly. The cow on the track stopped chewing but didn't look up.

"If we can make it look up, perhaps it will see the other cows going back to their field and follow them," suggested Dani.

"I don't think we're loud enough," shrugged Asha.

Hmm ... wondered Dani. How can I make it hear us? The express train will be here soon ...

Chapter 4

My microphone! Dani thought.

She leant out of the window and raised it to her mouth.

"MOOOOOOOO!" she bellowed.

The cow looked up with a start. Then it spotted the rest of the herd in the field and plodded off the track to follow them.

"Hurray!" cheered Dani. Tai updated the passengers.

Asha radioed the signaller. "We're clear to move … and should make it off the single track just in time."

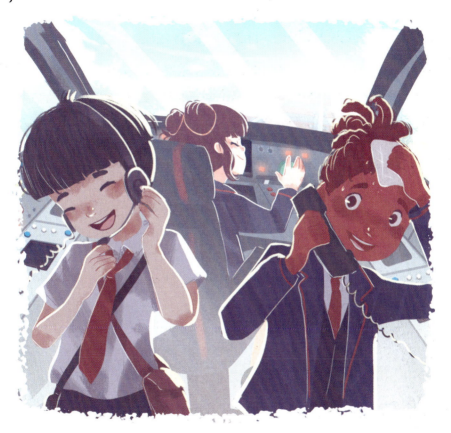

As Dani pulled the lever to get the train moving, something on the path next to the field caught her eye.

Two hikers! They must have gone through the gate and left it open. That's how the cows had got on to the track.

Dani waited until the train was level with them. Then she pulled out her microphone again.

"Excuse me!" Dani called out. "Could you shut the gate, please? We don't want the cows on the track again."

The hikers nodded apologetically and hurried back to close the gate.

"Full speed ahead, Dani," said Asha. "We need to make up the lost time!"

Dani's train arrived at the station bang on time. The passengers cheered.

"I was wrong about your microphone," said Asha. "You did need it, after all."

"You can keep it," laughed Dani, "in case you need to *moooooove* anything else from the tracks."

"It was your quick thinking that saved the day," said Asha, handing the microphone to Dani.

As Dani took it from Asha, she felt a tingle in her hand. Then her arm. Then her whole body started spinning and tumbling, away from the train station ...

Chapter 5

When the spinning stopped, Dani found herself back in the spare bedroom. She put the microphone in the toy box and closed the lid.

"Being a train driver was fantastic!" she told Tara. "I had to keep everything on time and on track – not easy when there's a cow blocking your way and danger coming down the line."

"I wonder what the toy box will train you up for next time?" laughed Tara. "All aboard for non-stop adventure!"

Dani's emotional journey

Ideas for reading

Written by Clare Dowdall, PhD
Lecturer and Primary Literacy Consultant

Reading objectives:
- discuss the sequence of events in books and how items of information are related
- draw on what they already know or on background information and vocabulary provided by the teacher
- check that the text makes sense to them as they read and correct inaccurate reading
- predict what might happen on the basis of what has been read so far

Spoken language objectives:
- maintain attention and participate actively in collaborative conversations, staying on topic and initiating and responding to comments
- gain, maintain and monitor the interest of the listener(s)

Curriculum links: PSHE: Health and wellbeing; Feelings

Interest words: microphone, depart, signal, panic, bellowed, radioed, worried, unsure, relieved

Resources: paper and pencils; ICT for research

Build a context for reading
- Look at the front cover and read the title. Ask a volunteer to explain what talented means, and to give an example of a talent, and someone who is talented.
- As a group, create a list of the skills and talents that a train driver might need.
- Turn to the blurb and read it aloud. Ask children to predict what the danger may be, and check that they understand the phrase down the line.

Understand and apply reading strategies
- Read pp2-3 to the children. Remind children that they know from the blurb that Dani is going to be a train driver, and that something will block the train line. Ask them to predict what the microphone might be used for in Dani's adventure.